VULNERABLE
HUMAN

Pawankumar Rai

© **Pawankumar Rai 2023**

All rights reserved

All rights reserved by author. No part of this publication may be reproduced, stored in a retrieval system or transmitted in any form or by any means, electronic, mechanical, photocopying, recording or otherwise, without the prior permission of the author.

Although every precaution has been taken to verify the accuracy of the information contained herein, the author and publisher assume no responsibility for any errors or omissions. No liability is assumed for damages that may result from the use of information contained within.

First Published in January 2023

ISBN: 978-93-5704-889-7

BLUEROSE PUBLISHERS

www.BlueRoseONE.com

info@bluerosepublishers.com

+91 8882 898 898

Cover Design:
Pawankumar Rai and Yash

Reviewed and Edited By:
Srishti Mehrotra

Typographic Design:
Tanya Raj Upadhyay

Distributed by: BlueRose, Amazon, Flipkart

"The entire world is spending billions to persuade men that they should be ashamed to be men rather than unerring artificial intelligence machines. However, they overlook the fact that only foolish and the dead are incapable of changing their views. Fools aren't going to do it and dead men are unable to do so."

Pawankumar Rai

(*Researcher by profession, writer by heart*)

"This book is dedicated to my friends and relatives without whom this book would have been completed five years earlier."

*

The first Chakra was probably the topic of more amateur astronomy observations than any other single object in the cosmos during its three-year lifespan. When a call for witnesses to the accident that destroyed the space station was made, almost 280 reports came in.

Fortunately, it was on the night side of the Earth at the time, and in a position where the sun shone brightly. Two of the observers' ten-inch mirrors were equipped with movie cameras. One of these had an unsatisfactory film, while the other had a whole record of the incident, from the *Vikram's* first approach through the pilot's bumbling attempt to correct course to the fatal crash.

For a few seconds, the scene was lost as the wreckage drifted out of the field. The observer, however, had been looking via a small pilot scope and had the foresight to pan by hand to catch most of the remaining fall that was visible over his horizon as the Chakra and the Vikram's locked fragments continued their slow, spiral approach to Earth.

By the time this picture was completed, news of the calamity had already spread throughout the government.

Bhaskar, the Chakra's radio operator, had been conversing with Prasoon, the Vikram's radio operator. All of their conversations were taped as a matter of course, and part of it was retrieved following the crash and played back throughout the investigation.

"and, get this," Prasoon said, "my kid just turned five last week, and I've already got him working on quadratic equations." To beat that one, you'll have to put in some effort."

"It doesn't matter," Bhaskar said. "You're aware of how quickly these baby brain compartments deteriorate. Take him fishing and let him forget about it for a time. Hey, what the hell is going on here? In the control room, you've got a truck driver? I just noticed you out of the port, and you appear to be right on top of us!"

"Deva, I'm not sure. That's how it's been since we cleared Dhanush (the spaceport). Sometimes I get the impression that this guy Khan was trained in a truck the way he is— Hell, he's on the wrong side of the Chakra! The orders to go to the east turret were transmitted to me. He was the one who acknowledged them-"

"Prasoon! We're going to hit! I can see you outside the harbour!"

The shattering, grinding scream of colliding metal ripped the words apart. Then, a split second later, the explosion of a fuel tank.

"Prasoon!"

"Yes, Bhaskar, I'm here. The lights have gone out. Power is still on in the event of an emergency. If you still have a rig, take the emergency exit. I'll be there for you-"

Bhaskar went on to the emergency channel, which was always monitored, and dialled Space Command Base. He said, "Chakra was just rammed by Vikram." "Loss of orbital velocity is a possibility. The extent of the damage is uncertain."

Lieutenant Yashashvi, who was on duty at the Base, had just returned from a three-day leave and was still getting back into the swing of things. His face flushed as he looked at the radar tracking screen and saw the irregular form there, just out of the centering circle. It wasn't a joke.

He said, "You're dropping."

"The orbital velocity has to be reduced. Could you please make a correction?"

"I am unable to make contact with the bridge," Bhaskar explained. "All commands should be alerted, and the crash point should be calculated. Keep an eye on everything."

It was discovered that the bridge, as well as a third of the station, had been completely destroyed. Captain Surya, on the other hand, had been spared because he was on inspection in the station's other sector. Bhaskar was able to get the communication lines repatched, so he got on right away.

He yelled, "Emergency red!" "All stations are required to report!"

The surviving crew chiefs reported the conditions in their sections one by one. And after they were done, they all realised their chances of surviving were little to none. Surya gave the following command: "Make contact with the base. Request that the crash point be plotted."

Bhaskar replied, "Done, sir."

"In the radio room, a command post will be built. On order, the emergencysteering process will begin. All taxi craft are men."

Everything was on the recordings that were saved. Everything was done to the best of human ability by desperate men.

***

By the time Bhaskar contacted Captain Surya, the base commander, General Bakshi, was in the communications and tracking room.

At the table, he took up the microphone. Lieutenant Yashashvi was ordered to "plug me in to the station."

He got Bhaskar first, but the radio operator immediately switched Captain Surya on as he entered the radio room. In a hushed voice, General Bakshi murmured, "Hello, Mitra."

Captain Surya replied, "Yes Biswas—" "I'm delighted you showed up. Does it appear to be in a horrible state?"

"The orbital velocity has decreased by 2%. For the past eight minutes, you've been plummeting."

"That's not good. I've manned all of the steering stations, but only about a third of them are still operational. We're also relying on cabs for assistance. But we haven't been able to get Vikram to move. It consumes over half of our available energy due to its inertia."

"Couldn't you go into orbit with a burst from Vikram's tubes?"

"Manu has a team of people working on it. However, his controls have been removed, and his fuel tanks have been unlocked. Even if we could get their rockets to work, there's a good chance we wouldn't be able to get the thrust in the appropriate direction. Our only hope is to use our own rockets to tear the spacecraft free from the station."

The higher the massed wreckage's orbital velocity needs were as it got closer to Earth. General Bakshi sat with his eyes on the tracking scope and the words of his friend in his ear while the workers frantically did their jobs. Captain Surya's precise command to the men in the station and those attempting to liberate the ship drew his attention. The failure to liberate the Vikram was repeatedly reported to General Bakshi. As the station's fuel supply ran short, he obeyed Surya's orders to transfer fuel from the ship to the station. He kept an eye on the spot on the tracking scope as it continued to move.

Then he turned around as a lieutenant approached him with a sheet of calculations in his hand. "Sir, the current rate of decline suggests a crash point in the Bay of Bengal region."

The General's face tightened as he grabbed the paper. Surya remarked, "Biswas, did I understand you correctly? Is it the Bengal region?"

"Yes."

"We'll have to do everything we can to prevent it from happening there. I'm going to order the missiles to be turned off right now. As we approach Earth, we would have saved enough fuel to try some last-minute steering."

"No!" General Bakshi was in tears. "Make use of it right now! It will have the same effect as before. Dismantle the chambers! Return to orbit!"

"We're not going to make it," Surya admitted gently.

"We've gained-forward velocity, but I'm willing to bet that at this orbit, your computers will show us to be less than four percent below requirements. As we free fall from our current point, try to spot our collision as precisely as possible. If we come close to a city, we'll use remaining fuel for last-minute steering."

The General became silent as he listened to the comments from the soldiers incharge of the rockets, who were well aware that with the closing of their fuel valves, their own lives were also coming to an end.

Bakshi finally stated, "We'll want a testimonial account for the investigation." "Get the cops in charge on the circuit—but first, Mitra—"

Before Captain Mitra, Surya began speaking in hushed tones, there was a brief pause. Finally, he questioned, "What is there to say?"

"There will be no need for an investigation."

"Right now, I can tell you everything you need to know—at least all you'll ever learn. Your decision will be the same as that of hundreds of thousands of other investigating boards before you: Pilot Error."

"Error due to human!"

That's how the first Chakra and the Vikram died. Me and Manu are not sure why this happened. Neither does any of the other men that are with us up here. Those who were in the control room with Khan are no longer alive, but they didn't know anything more than we do.

Khan, we spent a million dollars teaching him. We thought he was the finest we could come up with. We tested his reflexes, IQ, and blood composition until we thought we knew every molecule in his body's function and capabilities. Then, in a fraction of a second, he makes a moronic judgement, fumbling when precision was required. "

"What exactly did he do?" Bakshi inquired softly.

"The Surya turret is where we usually approach. Because of maintenance on the other end of the hub, he had been told to travel to the east side this time. Khan had seen the directives and had acknowledged them.

They must have escaped his mind as he approached the Chakra, for he ended up on the Surya side. Then he remembered and attempted to correct himself.

"Everything had to have gone wrong at that point. To begin with, the decision was a miscalculation. Yes, it's the wrong attitude. But attempting such a complex manoeuvre so close to the station was suicide. He rammed the Vikram into the Chakra at a 45-degree angle with his side jets, trapping the ship between the wreckage of the rim and the spokes' girders."

"Was there any previous evidence of pilot instability that you were aware of? Manu can give us a better answer, but we need to know if you were aware of anything."

"No, it's not true! Khan was checked out three days prior to the flight's departure. As far as any of our methods of evaluation went, he was fine. As right as any guy could possibly be-

"Biswas, pay attention to what I'm saying. Remember how we spoke about having a Chakra up here and ships taking off for the Moon and Mars when we were back at White Sands?"

"I recall," General Bakshi answered softly.

"We've got a piece of that dream, to be sure. But there will never be any more, and what we have will crumble until we address the one flaw we've never addressed adequately. You'll keep failing as long as men like Khan can demolish two decades of work and billions of rupees worth of engineering infrastructure.

"All of this is destroyed by one man's stupid, moronic error, as if it had never been."

"A plane crashes on the ground; the board chalks it up to pilot mistake, and the planes continue to fly. That's not possible out here! The price is far too high. Putting this mountain of machinery and effort in the hands of guys we may never be sure of is a huge risk.

You believe you know who they are, and you try everything you can to learn more about them. "However, you simply don't know."

"We've overcome every other technical stumbling block on our path. Why haven't we figured it out yet?

We've figured out how to build a machine that will work predictably, and when it doesn't, we'll be able to provide enough feedback alerts and correctors, as well as pinpoint the source of the issue.

"We can't do anything with a man."

"In the end, we have no choice but to accept him on the basis of trust."

An error by human will result in the deaths of several hundred men.

Give us a memorial!

Learn why males make mistakes. Make a way to keep them away from it. Do that, and our deaths will be a minor inconvenience!

These were the last words spoken by a man who had passed away. In the committee rooms and investigative chambers, they were repeatedly heard. They were printed and aired all across the world, allowing General Bakshi to carry out what would become a flaming crusade.

If those words hadn't been shouted by a dying man as a screeching, white-hot mass descended through the skies, eventually landing in the Indian Ocean's waters, he would have most likely failed.

Surya's rocket fuel, which he had so carefully conserved, was not required to guide the wreckage past the city of Bengal. The Chakra and the Vikram were doomed the moment Khan, the ship's pilot, decided to change the ship's position in relation to the station.

***

When the secretary wasn't looking, Dr. Batra brushed the palms of his hands against his pant legs in the anteroom of the Base Commander's office, and tasted the dryness that scorched the membrane of his lips.

He was recalled by the secretary. She was most likely the one who read his severance papers and was well aware of Bakshi's decision to fire him.

She was probably wondering why the General had called him back after that traumatic experience, just as Batra was.

But he was fairly certain he knew. If he was correct, it was a once-in-a-lifetime opportunity, and he couldn't afford to squander it.

When she heard a buzz on the intercom, she turned around. "You may go in now," she added with a smile.

"Thanks." He stood up and urged his nervousness to forget about the last time he went through the door he was about to walk through. General Bakshi was little more than the Base Commander, and if Batra was fired again, he would be no worse off than he was now.

Bakshi raised his head, a grim smile forming at the corners of his mouth. He shook hands and motioned to a chair near the desk, before returning to his place behind it. "Despite our prior disputes, you know why I called."

Batra took a moment to think. He didn't want to express his fear—or his optimism—so he evaluated the possible responses and said, "It's this crash thing—and Captain Surya's appeal?"

"Would there be anything else?"

"It means a lot to me that you thought of me."

"Believe me when I say there's nothing personal at stake! I'd have called someone else a thousand times over—anyone else—but no one can accomplish the job like you."
"Thanks."

"Please don't thank me. I expect there will still be significant disagreements between us on the project's basic objectives. But I don't want to have to fire you again once we get started."

"What is the nature of this project, and what are its objectives?" Batra asked. Please fill me in on the specifics."

"You're not going to supply any specifics beyond what you've read and heard. The goal is to find a type of guy who will prevent future Mitra Suryas from dying in the same way as those aboard the Chakra did."

"What kind of man do you think he is?" Batra inquired.

"One who will put an end to the terrible verdict that has been handed down in tens of thousands of accident and disaster investigations: human mistake." We're going to uncover a type of man that can be counted on to perform flawlessly. One who can accomplish a complex work according to a well-defined technique an endless number of times without deviating from the norm."

Batra's eyes were narrowed as he looked at the General. He needed to have a clear understanding with Bakshi now, despite his nearly excruciating desire to have the appointment to head up this Project. He had no choice but to take chances in order to make himself completely clear.

He explained, "For untold thousands of years, the human race has made every effort to achieve perfection but has never succeeded. Now you propose bringing together all the money in the world, as well as all the wits, and demand a perfect man! He is required by the Indian Space Command!"

"Exactly." As he returned Batra's steady gaze, General Bakshi's face tightened. "No other technical issue has ever been able to withstand such an assault. There's no reason for this one to be different. And the problem must be solved, or we will be forced to quit space just as we are approaching the edge, receiving our first actual view of it."

"General," Batra replied slowly, "your world is such a straightforward, uncomplicated place." "You're looking for a man with two heads, four arms, and a tail. Place your order now! "Here we go!" "That's how you operated five years ago when I set up your basic personnel programme. It didn't work then, and it isn't going to work today."

The General's visage became gloomy. "It'll work out. Because it has to be done. Men are compelled to reach for the stars. And they'll adapt to whatever shape, size, or ability is required to achieve that goal.

They've accomplished everything else they've ever set out to accomplish-life sprung from the water because it had bravery. Men emerged from their cavesand swept across the plains and seas, claiming the entire Earth and transformingit into what it is today—all because they had the bravery to do it.

"However, courage isn't enough to get to space. We need a new type of man, one we haven't seen before. He's an iron man who's forgotten what it's like to be human. He's a machine that can repeat the same complicated procedure over and over without making an error. He's more dependable and durable than any of our previous equipment.

"I'm not sure where we'll find him, but he can be discovered, and you'll find him because, like me, you think that Man's frontier should never be closed. And because, despite your cynicism, you still understand what it means to have a responsibility towards your society and race.

There is no way you could refuse, so I've already taken procedures to make your appointment official."

"You must also have prepared yourself to accept me with the core concept that must lead me in this situation," Batra continued. And this Project, in my opinion, must fail. It has no chance of succeeding. The man you're looking for doesn't exist. A man who makes no mistakes is a dead man.

"Any live person is bound to make mistakes. Making an approach, correcting for errors, approaching again, then correcting once more is the learning process. It's the only way to gain knowledge."

"The General took a deep breath and paused. "I don't know anything about that," he finally said. "You already know what I'm looking for." Even if some of what you say is true, there's no reason why what you've learned can't be put into practice without error. I may have to put up with it, but if you don't spend three months looking for reasons why the project can't succeed, you'll save yourself and all of us a lot of time."

He stood up, as if all that could possibly be said had already been spoken. "Let's go have a look at your lab space."

They strolled across the yard from the administration building to a big laboratory that had been stripped down to the bare floor and walls in the scorching heat of the Thar Desert. Batra's sense of insecurity had returned. But only for a split second. He'd almost insulted the General by telling him he had no intention of making the iron hanuman that Space Command was considering. And he hadn't been kicked out yet. They must have a strong desire for him!

He had no concerns about accepting the position at this time. General Bakshi had been forewarned and was aware of Batra's intents and hopes.

The General said, "You can build your staff as big as you need it."

"This project takes precedence above all others. We have the technology to travel to space. Men are required by the machines."

"You can have anybody you want and do whatever you want with them. We hope you can put them back together in reasonable condition, but it isn't critical."

Batra walked around the barren room, which would do as office space. He said, "All right."

"Consider this the start of Project Hanuman. Remember, there's no way I'm going to discover a solution in a perfect human being. I'll seek out whatever answers are available. If you have any concerns to the way I'm working with those terms, please express them now. I don't want to get fired again while the project is still in progress."

"You will not be. You'll figure out a method to provide us with what we require. I'd like you to come down to the far end of the building and meet a man who will be working with you closely."

General Bakshi led Batra towards the sounds of action in the distance. They walked inside a spacious room where musical instruments were being put up. As they walked in, a tall, skinny, dark-haired man approached them.

"Dr. Dhruv Khatri, instrument and electronics expert," the General continued. Dr. Batra is the country's leading expert on psychology and psychometric analysis.

"Your instrument man will be Dr. Khatri. He'll develop and construct whatever specialised equipment your research necessitates. Please let me know as soon as possible what furnishings and assistants you'll require."

He abandoned them in the practically empty room. They could see his stiff form march back to his own office through the window.

Khatri shifted his weight and greeted Batra with a smile. "I suppose I should tell you that the General has given me a full briefing on your likely reaction to the project. I'm only inquisitive enough to find out if he's correct."

"I think the General and I understand one other," Batra remarked. "He's well aware that I despise his solution-oriented approach to an issue of human behaviour. But he knows I'll take his money and put it in the largest, most comprehensive study of human behaviour ever undertaken using psychometric analysis."

"It should be enough to buy gold fringed couches for all of the country's experts."

Batra's brows furrowed. "If you're like that, why are you joining me?" He inquired.

"Because I, too, have a vested interest in this! I share the General's desire to see the matter resolved. And I believe it is solvable. "But not in this manner!"

"There is only one method to create men with exceptional ability. Appropriate training method. Self-discipline and training that is harsh and cruel. After Bakshi sees the failure you plan to manufacture for him, I'll persuade him of it."

"That shouldn't be difficult," Batra added. "It is the General's personal opinion. The project's sole purpose is to put that viewpoint into action "But let's be clear about what I'm trying to do. For every dollar spent on research, I intend to provide honest value. I intend to find information that will help the Command provide better spacemen—and to give Captain Surya the monument he requested!"

***

Batra stood alone in his hotel room that night, staring out the window into the desert. A bright glow in the sky marked the location of Space Command Base beyond the far hills. He looked at it, thinking of the immensity of what was being produced for the world in that remote outpost. Now was his moment to show that manhood was a quality to be proud of, that machines could be constructed, junked, and rebuilt, but that a man's existence was unique in the universe and could never be replaced once crushed.

He'd worked for years to understand Man's fundamental nature and what separates him from the mechanical. He'd anticipated that he'd never be able to achieve his aim due to a lack of funds.

Then Bakshi appeared, offering him the entire universe in exchange for achieving a hazy goal that Space Command had no idea was unattainable.

That money was going to be spent by someone. Batra rationalised, with a clear conscience, that it could just as well be on him. He'd make sure the country got good value for its money, even if it wasn't exactly what the Space Command had hoped for.

Khatri was going to be a formidable opponent. Batra wished the General had allowed him choose to his own technical director, but the two men clearly communicated well. They were similar in their approaches to human performance in their respective domains. Make a guy come to heel like a hesitant hound by whipping him into line. You can beat him, shape him, and twist him into the shape you wish.

Put him in his place. That was the answer to everything, the magic word.

Batra turned away from the window, drawing the curtains on the Base's skyglow, disgusted.

Error due to human!

When will Man stop making this most colossal of all blunders? When would he stop seeing himself and his peers as brutish monsters who needed to be beaten into submission?

He needed to find the right answer before Bakshi and his ilk discovered some thin support for the one they'd already decided on.

He got up and looked at the clock, concluding that he did, in fact, want dinner. He'd send a message to Shetty and the kids the next day, telling them to collect their belongings and be ready to go. He'd call tonight, no. She had a right to know the outcome of his interview right away.

The dining room was almost empty. While waiting, he placed an order absently and clipped the speaker of his small personal radio behind his ear. He rarely used it, but there was a sense of solitude in the desert that made him seize any contact with the bright, distant world almost compulsively. The music was monotonous, and the news was uninteresting. When his order arrived, he was about to switch it off.

The wine was terrible, but the steak was excellent, so Batra thought it was about even. He pressed his finger against the radio switch once more. The newscaster's voice took on a hammering, urgent tone. "The repercussions of the world's first space station's recent accident are still being felt," he stated. "There are rumblings of opposition to the construction of a new Chakra in various areas. They've grown to the size of a roar now.

"The prominent Times of Bharat declares that any restoration of the Chakra is 'unqualifiedly opposed.' The structure's three-year existence established beyond a shadow of a doubt its complete lack of utility. Now that it has fallen to Earth, it reveals the threat that its existence poses to every city on the planet."

"Senator Deshmukh is in agreement with these sentiments. 'It was complete stupidity to invest billions of dollars to build this Vajra of Indra in the sky of the entire world in the first place'. I recommend that our government go on record as denying any future plans to reconstruct such a threat to the peace and well-being of nations who are now on the verge of achieving the understanding and friendship that they have yearned for so long."

It was turned off by Batra. While the Chakra was falling toward the city of Bengal, he remembered the hours of global turmoil. In a panic, the whole Bay Area population attempted to flee, but there was no time. The bridges were jammed, and several delirious drivers exited their vehicles and leapt into the waters below.

The computers decreased their circle of error as the wreckage approached Earth, until it was finally assured that the city would not be hit. However, the harm had already been done. Fear remained, and it was now congealing into a furious determination to prevent the construction of another Chakra.

Batra completed his breakfast, pondering the implications for the plans to construct a new Chakra and Project Hanuman. Perhaps Congress would be so enraged that it would cut off all funding to the Project.

In a moment of exhaustion, he pondered if this would not, after all, be an unmixed blessing.

***

The next three days were spent communicating with members of his trade by telephone and telegraph as he sought to hire a staff.

Shetty and the kids arrived on Friday. The laboratory furniture had been installed by the end of the following week, and the first wave of potential employees had arrived to see what Hanuman was all about. Khatri had been working as well, assembling his own team and putting together rudimentary equipment.

Batra had the impression that they were setting up opposing camps on the same exploratory site. Until Khatri approached him a few days later, he attempted to convince himself that it was entirely crazy.

"You're bringing quite a bunch in here," the technician observed. "If you want to find couch room for all your boys, you'll have to take Bakshi up on his offer of new structures."

"That's why you're here," Batra gently offered, "to get rid of couches."

"Right." Khatri smiled and nodded. "A metre can do twice as well as a couch at everything."

"Both are sometimes required. You seem to have forgotten that psychometry is my area of expertise."

"No, I'm not forgetting," Khatri stated emphatically. "That is, however, what makes it so difficult for me to figure out. You're striving to bridge two fields that are diametrically opposed: science and humanities. Man acts either like a machine or like a creature with erratic emotions. You must suppress the other in order to function as one."

"I'll place a tiny wager on you. On Hanuman, we'll have to collaborate and coordinate all of our methods and outcomes. But I'm willing to wager that the ultimate answer comes from the perspective of a purely mechanical guy, devoid of any other responses and motivations."

"I'll take it!" Batra murmured a glum smile on his face. "I'm not sure how much of an answer we'll get, but I'm sure it won't be that!"

"Let's imagine there's a small celebratory meal for the entire crew once Hanuman is finished. There's nothing cheesy about it, either!"

They shook their heads. After that, Batra was relieved that the situation had transpired. There was no doubt in

Khatri's mind about the direction in which he would take his work.

***

Batra summoned the first meeting of his staff leaders four weeks to the day after stepping into Bakshi's office. Invitations to the General and Khatri were deleted on purpose. He intended for this initial gathering to be a family affair.

As he stood up in front of the group for the first time, he felt a little unsteady in the knees.

"I'm not going to tell you anything you don't already know," Batra stated gently.

"You're all aware of the events that led to the creation of Project Hanuman." I'm sure you've noticed the two fundamental fallacies that the Space Command has made: first, that an errorless man is feasible, and second, that true scientific discovery can be achieved entirely on command.

General Bakshi understands that we believe these assumptions are incorrect, but he also understands that our professional integrity requires us to pursue a route that he believes will lead to success.

"We also understand that we aren't here to create or construct anything that doesn't already exist. Our bosses and some of our coworkers, on the other hand, seem to expect us to do just that.

"However, we can all agree that the majority of Man's potential has yet to be uncovered. And for those of us who have wished for a way to comprehend that potential, this Project is a dream come true. If we do not take full advantage of it, we will gain a century of condemnation for our profession.

"Space Command has already established that a machine's robotic reflexes can strip a man of his humanity and push him to a totally mechanical state."

Let there be no doubt: we've been sent here to corroborate that conclusion. Unless we can give a clean-cut explanation and proofs of the thing that most of us believe: that the essence of Man is more than a piece of technology or a collection of bio-chemical reactions, we will legitimise it by default.

"Our understanding of the mind and of man is being put to the test. If we fail, we give our approval to a dogma that will extend from space technology to the rest of our society, imprisoning Man in an iron mould that will last for decades.

While we have been hired and will purportedly focus on building an error-free man, our primary goal must be to prove Man's humanity!"

He awaited their response. A missile roared into the air outside the station, far across the vast desert. They waited till the noise stopped.

Professor Sakchham Shukla rose to his feet. "There isn't a single human being alive who hasn't heard or read Captain Surya's appeal. They'll be waiting for the day when the errorless man he requested will appear, striding out our laboratories like a robot.

"Do you imply we have to go against the Project's stated goals? Isn't it possible to come up with a system of training that will accomplish the objectives the Space Command requires in a different way?"

"We are not opposing Space Command's demand for more capable soldiers for its ships," Batra explained. "We're merely battling against the erroneous conclusions they've already drawn about the nature of such persons.

"The issue of human mistake must be addressed. We understand what role it plays in the learning process. In a learnt process, we must discover the rationale for its existence. We need to figure out exactly what training entails.

"We have to ask how we know when we've made a mistake." When a spaceship collides with a fixed orbit station, it is clear. But what about the more nuanced instances, where the outcomes are less dramatic or delayed for an extended period of time-?

"The most important thing to remember at this stage is that our primary goal is to prevent any erroneous confirmation of the notion that Man is nothing more than a malfunctioning machine that will earn value after he has been tinkered with enough to blend in with the gears and vacuum tubes. And in order to accomplish this, we must first learn of his genuine nature."

***

General Bakshi paid his first visit to Hanuman two weeks after the project began. The soldier's face was more wrinkled and his eyes more tired than Batra remembered them being.

"You appear to have things under control," he observed. "Can you provide us some concrete outcomes as soon as possible?"

"Results! We've only recently begun housekeeping. We'll know where to start a focused search for what you want to know in a year, maybe two."

The General slowly shook his head, his gaze remaining fixed on Batra's. "You won't have anything close to a year. You don't have time to go over each line of research one by one. Run them all at the same time—a thousand at a time if you wish. Why do you believe you have the budget you do?"

"Threading a needle—or analysing a human person," Batra explained, "doesn't go much faster when a thousand men work on it than when there's only one."

"When there are a thousand needles to thread or brains to pluck, they do it. And that's exactly what we're up against. We need a large number of the kind of men we've been discussing, and we need them now!"

"We need to figure out how to obtain the first one," says the group.

"And you don't have as much time as we thought you did when Hanuman first appeared. They're attempting to shut us down.

"We hadn't intended to develop another Chakra right once, not until we'd worked out some design issues and gotten some feedback from Hanuman.

"All of that has now been abandoned. We've got orders from New Delhi to start building a second Chakra right now, using the same plans as the first. The construction of the structures has already begun."

"I don't get it," Batra remarked.

"If we don't get another one up there in the next few weeks, the public's hysteria will likely prevent us from ever putting one up there again. We must act now, while we still have authority, before the crackpots persuade Congress to deprive us of it. And by the time it's finished, I'd like some men to help me put it together. Men who can be trusted not to jeopardise it as soon as their clumsy feet get on board. I'm after them, Batra, and I'm going to get them. That's a formal request!"

Although the General stood up, Batra remained seated. "You know you can't obtain them that way," the latter said. "As I've told you previously, we'll do everything we can."

"I believe you will now do a lot more. That was a powerful speech you gave to your guys a few weeks ago. We'll 'ostensibly labour at the task of building an errorless individual,' as you put it, I suppose. Batra, you're going to do a lot more than just nominally work on it. How much do you think you'll be able to getaway with?"

Batra sat in his chair, motionless. His lips were the only thing that moved. "So you got a report on our briefing? I think it was clear enough to convey the rest of what I said, namely, that my primary goal was not to create human robots, but to establish man's humanity."

Bakshi drew in closer, his fists resting on the desk's top. "Man's humanity will be damned! We want guys who have forgotten they were ever human, men of metal and electrons, as I already stated. You wouldn't be here another minute if I didn't believe you were the only man in the country capable of doing it. You, on the other hand, can and will succeed.

"If you undermine Hanuman, your brief lecture is enough to damage your career in any area you try to go to. After that declaration of intent to sabotage the Project your government entrusted you with and which you agreed to carry out, who do you think would trust you with any kind of research?

"Unless you give me what I've asked for, Batra, you're finished, thoroughly washed up in your own profession! I'm no longer willing to make promises. From now on, the only assurance you can provide me is results! I'm after those folks, and I'm after them now!"

***

Professor Sakchham sat opposite from Batra in the administration office, listening intently as he relayed Bakshi's visit and requests.

"We're in a tight spot, and we have to press both ways," Batra added. "If the Base is destroyed, Hanuman will perish with it, and we will have missed a once-in-a-lifetime opportunity. So we need to do two things: actively promote the rebuilding of the Chakra, and devise a display that will persuade Bakshi that Hanuman is giving him what he desires. It will mean deviating from our primary goals, but it is required in order to have a project at all. I'd prefer you to lead the charge."

Sakchham said slowly, "It'll be a waste of time." "I'm not sure if we'll ever be able to get back on track."

"We'll have to take a chance," Batra remarked. "I don't want you to think I'm dragging you down a rabbit hole, but I believe you're the best man for coming up with something we can sell Bakshi-while we try to do some serious research on some honest goals."

"Through shock and terror, as well as pain and discomfort, we can follow the traditional lines of so-called training-brute conditioning. In that regard, the majority of the males here are already well anaesthetized. Their level of breakdown is quite high."

"Khan was the highest," Batra explained, "and he broke." However, continue to work in that direction. Perhaps we can find a method to make the conditioning armour thicker. Simultaneously, let us push as hard as we can for a genuine research into the nature of error. For the time being, we'll ignore the Project's larger goals until we know it's safe."

Sakchham agreed grudgingly, fearful that they would soon be reduced to simply personnel counsellors. Batra dialled Bakshi's number as soon as he left.

He said, "I've got a suggestion." "Let's not get into a defensive stance over this. Why don't you recommend that Space Command be investigated by the Senate?"

"Are you insane? Why should we want people to come out here and take our bones apart before burying them?"

"Remember, we have a narrative to tell them? We have Hanuman, who will generate a man capable of facing the hazards of space for the first time in human history. And then there's that bravery storey you told me about. I believe that would be acceptable to them. We'd be ahead of the game if we seized theinitiative instead of waiting for it to roll over us."

Bakshi took a long gap before speaking again. "I'm not sure what you're tryingto accomplish," he finally said. "I know you're not serious about what you're saying-"

"But," Batra stated solemnly, "I do mean it." "I'd like to see Hanuman saved, and you'd like to see the Chakra. It's essentially the same thing."

"You might be correct. It's possible that you're telling the truth. I'll think about it some more."

***

A teenage engineer-soldier named Igbal was in command of the rocket crews and the take-off stand. During his first week at Base, Batra had met him. His enthusiasm for Project Hanuman was contagious.

Batra drove a jeep over to the stand after speaking with Bakshi and found Iqbal. The engineer was in charge of a large rocket's fueling operation.

"Doc Batra!" Iqbal was ecstatic. "How's it doing with your head shrinkers crew? We're almost ready for your new generation of pilots."

"What do you mean?".

"This is the nucleus ship. She'll launch into space tonight with the first shipment of supplies and instruments in preparation for the new Chakra. We're going to require your soldiers as soon as possible."

"That's why I've come to speak with you. Do you have a few minutes to spare?"

"Sure." Iqbal took him to the office, where the whining of the fuel pumps was muted. "Can you tell us what we can do for you?"

"I had a question about Khan. Did you know him very well?" "Buddies. It was as simple as that." Igbal made a cross with his fingers.

"What do you believe went wrong? I know it's all been discussed in the investigations, but I'm curious about your personal thoughts on him."

Iqbal's cheeks flushed, and he averted his gaze for a time. He described Khan as "as fine a guy as they come." "In a crisis, though, he was just a frail sister. That isn't to say he didn't have a lot on his plate, "Iqbal countered with a defensive remark."

"He was a greater pilot than most of us will ever be, but he was just like the rest of us a human being."

"What do you mean when you say 'human'?"

"Weakness, softness, failure when things get tough—all these things we have to be aware of every minute we're living."

"I assume it you don't think much of people in general."

Iqbal took a step forward, his face solemn. "Listen, Doc, when you've spent as much time around ships as I have, you'll understand what Captain Surya meant."

The persons involved in the operation of any technological development have always been the weakest link. Our pilots and technicians are our greatest vulnerability in space flight. Set a machine on a course, and it'll keep going until it breaks down—and warn you before it does. You never know when a man is going to fail, and you have to be on the lookout for it every minute because he won't give you any notice.

"Imagine how it feels to be in our shoes!" We take command of machinery worth a few hundred million rupees, and we know that every single one of us is booby-trapped with a flaw that could explode at any time and destroy everything. We struggle to contain it and act as responsible instruments in the face of it. And we begin to despise ourselves as a result of our flaws.

"Khan was the same way. Every waking hour, he fought himself, knowing that he had a weakness for becoming confused in a stressful situation. It wasn't even something that showed up on the exams, yet he was the best man on the Base. But he knew it was there, just as we all know our closets are overflowing with skeletons we're trying to keep hidden."

"Do you fight your own battles like Khan?" Batra inquired.

"Sure."

"What would happen if you made a mistake and wrecked that ship on the stand?"

"That's all I'd have wanted. As long as I lived, I'd never get within ten miles of a missile base again. And there wouldn't be much reason to live-"

"Wouldn't it be nice to feel like you weren't always on the point of making a disastrous blunder?"

"Handling these ships with that kind of feeling inside him would be a rocketman's idea of nirvana."

"We're almost ready to start testing Hanuman, and I'd like you to be the first to assist us. Are you able to make it happen?"

"We're strung together like a ball of string trying to get the nucleus spacecraft into orbit. When you called, Bakshi gave us orders to leap, but I'll have to check on replacements for those of us you take. What kind of examination will you subject me to?"

"I'm curious as to how long it takes you to make a major blunder, and what happens if you do!"

***

Two days later, arrangements were made to begin this set of examinations. They were planned by Batra, and the equipment was produced by Khatri's crew.

However, Batra became increasingly aware of the outcry and public agitation against the Chakra before they began. Instead of dying out after a short outburstof rage, it was gaining traction across the country.

Swami, a rabble-rouser, planned a vehicle caravan to Space Command Base, where the members would stage a sit-in strike until assurances that no Chakra will be built again were granted. On the heels of this, an increasing number of Senators demanded a complete probe into the Base.

After witnessing Swami's revivalist-style request for a caravan of protest against the Base on the news, Batra met Sakchham. "This appears to be something that would be difficult to handle," Sakchham added. "It doesn't seem likely that the first Chakra's near-crash in Bengal is to blame for all this controversy."

"I don't believe it is," Batra said thoughtfully. "When a large ocean liner sinks, there are no frenzied demands that no further ships be built. Without this kind of reaction, the crash of an airship with a hundred people on board is accepted for what it is. I believe that the broadcasts and articles about Captain Surya's appeal have had a greater impact than Bakshi or anybody else planned.

"A sense of man's inferiority to his machines has been growing for a long time. Now, the Chakra event and the worldwide broadcast of Surya's final words have turned that inferiority into true terror. They don't want another Chakra to appear above their heads. They're scared that no man will ever be able to master such a machine."

This fear permeated not just the general populace, but also the men who were responsible for the ships' operation. As he returned to his own office, Batra realised that Iqbal was correct. To be in their shoes, facing the continual notion that they were lowly sad animals unfit to polish the gleaming hulls of their inventions, must be terrifying!

They were taught in the best military traditions, relying on brute might to overcome their deficiencies. Despite their training and customs, they had come to the conclusion that their own breakdown was unavoidable. What hope could such individuals have for the stars?

But where was the weakness in the whole thing? Where was the solution if notin men who were more like their own machines?

They needed a year or two to adequately handle the matter, yet a response was required within weeks!

The morning Iqbal was supposed to start his test runs, Batra arrived at the facility. He explained, "We're going on a complete crash-priority basis, with round-the-clock shifts." "It was a toss-up between closing Hanuman and putting everything we had on the new Chakra or leaving it open in the hopes of getting something out of it.

"I'm leaving it open for the time being, but keep in mind that every hour Iqbal or one of his men spends here is an hour away from the Chakra job." We didn't require your investigation suggestion. Many others had come up with the idea before you. In four or five days, the Senators will arrive. You are going to have a conversation with them.

You're going to tell them what you said you were going to say.

"Of certainly," she says. And how are you going to deal with Swami's entourage?"

Bakshi let out a loud yell. "We'll erect obstacles within ten miles of Base that they must not cross!"

"That isn't going to help," Batra cautioned. "I believe you should also allow me to prepare something for them."

"Forget about them! You'll be doing plenty if you take care of the Senators and the Project."

Iqbal arrived shortly after, apprehensive despite his best efforts to appear calm. When they transported him to Khatri's laboratory of intricate testing equipment, though, he felt at comfortable.

Batra pointed to a seat in the middle of the jumble of gear. "This resembles the landing technique of a rocket craft as closely as we've been able to get it," he stated. There are a total of 137 separate actions, observations, and judgments to consider.

You will be guided through the sequence by a voice recording, who will ask you to touch buttons and make adjustments to express your observations and replies.

When you've completed all of this to your satisfaction, turn off the tape and repeat for as many cycles as possible."

"How long do you think it will take? If he didn't have to sleep, a man could do that for a month."

"I believe you will be astonished. You'll keep going until the number of faults you've accumulated is so high that the entire procedure falls apart."

"To me, it still appears like a kid's game," Iqbal asserted. "Let's get this party started."

They carefully placed the electro-encephalograph recorder's many electrodes on his skull. Iqbal started the first cycle after turning on the tape instructor.

Batra, Khatri, Professor Sakchham, and two assistants sat behind the observation room's one-way glass, watching. The rocket engineer started off briskly, dismissing the minor steps needed of him and eager to go back to his duties at the take-off platform.

The instructions coming over the speaker differed from standard ship procedures in some ways, such as the things needed to record observations and responses. For a half-dozen cycles, Iqbal listened to these. He then turned off the tape and sat back to relax, knowing that he could get through the procedure for the rest of the day if necessary.

He watched the metres one by one, noting their information, making the necessary changes, adding compensations, waiting for results, checking and rechecking- "He'll go a long time," Khatri firmly predicted. "He has received excellent training. We might learn a few things if it breaks down."

"Khan, too, got top-notch training," Batra added. "His break point didn't appear to have any predecessors. I don't think Iqbal will be able to hold out for long."

After an hour, Iqbal's contemptuous expression had vanished, and he was moving with obvious ennui. He hadn't made a mistake yet, but there was a tinge of concern in his expression as he focused on the dials and levers.

At two and a half hours, Iqbal grabbed for a button and abruptly withdrew his hand. Then it darted out again, pressing down hard. He was making two such hesitations every cycle at three hours.

Sakchham remarked, "Not so good." "Not for a man who fights his own demons like Iqbal."

Khatri remained deafeningly silent, his gaze fixed on the swaying dials and graphs depicting the engineer's bodily state and reaction.

Iqbal's hand groped for a lever in the centre of the board at four and a half hours. However, it only made it about a third of the way. It suddenly froze in mid-air, as if paralysis had hit it. Iqbal looked at it with a look of bemusement. His cheeks flushed, and sweat beaded on his brow, as though from the physical struggle of attempting to reach the lever.

Batra took out a microphone and turned it on. He commanded, "Touch the lever." "Draw it in your direction."

Iqbal looked around nervously, but he finished the action. He sat for two minutes starring at the panels, his alarming eyes turning from green to yellow to red.

"Alarm red!" Batra yelled something into the microphone. "Of course!" said the speaker.

Iqbal turned and scanned the area with a hateful expression on his face, as if looking for the source of the noise. He started ripping the wires and connectors that were attached to his head and torso. He screamed, "To hell with the course!" "I'm getting out of here!"

The electrical harness was tossed towards the panels by him. He then stood in a state of additional paralysis before slumping onto the chair. He sat his arms and head on the instrument desk and sobbed uncontrollably.

Batra stowed the microphone and walked over to the front entrance. He said, "That's the end of that." "I'm hoping we have a decent track record. Iqbal may not want to go through it all over again."

Khatri was still staring at the sobbing engineer through the window. He whispered, "I don't understand." "What caused him to have a nervous breakdown for no apparent reason?"

***

The Base's best engineers went through the breakdown test one by one. Some, like Iqbal, had an emotional breakdown, while others simply ended in a whirlwind of uncertainty with lights flashing all over the panels. However, they all had a breakdown of some sort that could be quantified in a few hours.

The test was a guessing game. It was founded on the old and well-known notion that repeated tactile contact under command will quickly break down the body's motor responses. Batra wasn't sure if it would genuinely provide a fertile lead to the problem of error, but it seemed like the best option at the time.

Khatri, on the other hand, was taken aback by the men's reaction. He insisted on doing everything himself, adamant that no matter what happened, he would not give up. After six hours, the panel began to glow like a Christmas tree.

He ran the generated curves through an analyzer, and he paid special attention to his own. He called Batra with an excitement he couldn't contain in his voice after the end of a whole week of study on it.

He said, "It appears that you owe me that dinner." "We've found what we were looking for!" exclaims the group.

"Can you tell me what you're talking about?" Batra was adamant.

"We now have evidence that a human being is nothing more than a simple cybernetic device. It's a hoax that people have been trying to develop a mechanical man for so long. That's the only one available!"

"You're still not getting it." "Come over and have a look for yourself."

Batra left his office, puzzled and furious, and headed down to the analyzer laboratory. There, he discovered Khatri and his team, who were ecstatic.

Multiple recorder sheets were spread out on large tables and meticulously examined. Khatri led Batra to a series that was distinct from the others.

"At first, we didn't realise we had anything," Khatri explained. "The pulse had such a small amplitude that it was difficult to distinguish it from the background noise, but the analyzer revealed that it was continuously present under particular subject conditions."

"What conditions?" Batra inquired.

"At the very moment that you make a mistake! It happens between the decision to carry out an erroneous act and the triggering of the motor impulse that executes it, or between the decision to carry out an erroneous act and thetriggering of the motor impulse that executes it."

Batra smirked. "How can you be certain it doesn't happen at other times?"

"Because we've ran every set of charts through the analyzer, and this impulse appears nowhere else."

"It appears to be really intriguing," Batra added. "But why did you claim thatyou have proof that a human is nothing more than a cybernetic device? I'm not sure what this has to do with anything."

"I didn't tell you the whole thing," Khatri smugly admitted. "I should have clarified that the pulse occurred whenever there was a desire to commit an error. This intention was not always carried out."

"I'm not sure what you're talking about."

"That pulse is nothing more than a feedback pulse signalling the creation of an action matrix that is out of sync with the previously selected learning or intent pattern. It's a feedback alarm that warns that if the intended action is carried out, an error will occur.

When feedback is successfully delivered to the action matrix, a change is made until no feedback is received and the proper action is executed. An error occurs when feedback is prevented or disregarded.

That's all there is to it! Your complicated human is nothing more than a fairly complex cybernetic machine that runs entirely on feedback principles. Only when he stops acting like the cybernetic machine that he is, does he fail and break down!"

***

As he patted the lengthy strips of paper on the table, Khatri's eyes sparkled gleefully. Batra kept staring at the graphs in a surprised recognition as he followed his hand's motion. There had to be some blunder somewhere. Even if the statistics were right, Khatri's interpretation was incorrect. A feedback response mechanism—many thanks! If this is accurate, a vacuum tube structure could one day be designed to do anything a man could.

"I believe we'll put that supper off a little longer," Batra suggested. "The statistics are intriguing and, I'm sure, valuable, but I find it difficult to concur with your conclusions." He scolded himself for the stiltedness in his voice and his unjustified irritation of Khatri's continuous smug smirk.

"Take as much time as you like," Khatri continued, "but when you're done, you'll have the same answers I have." Man is nothing more than a machine. Our sole task today is to figure out why the feedback occasionally fails and get it back on track."

Batra returned to his office with the tapes and analyzer graphs.

He dialled Sakchham's number and informed him of Khatri's discovery. ""We don't need to worry about validating Space Command's pre-determined findings if this is accurate," he stated. It has already been accomplished."

As he sat down at the desk to check the charts, Dr. Sakchham appeared bewildered and a little scared. He looked up after an hour. He admitted, "It's true." "There's no getting around it. Take a look at what we've got—" He pointed to a section on each of the six charts he'd arranged.

"There was no attempt to correct after the first feedback impulse," he stated, "or, rather, there was a conscious effort to conceal the feedback." This resulted in a second, greater feedback, which resulted in more suppression and an amplification of the error at the same time. The outcome was a hunting effect with rising amplitude, similar to the needle of an undamped positive feedback autosyn indicator.

"And now for something completely different. In this situation, the hunting has a decreasing amplitude as a result of the feedback pulses correcting the effort. One pulse is insufficient; but, as the desire is brought into line with the taught pattern, they are administered with diminishing force.

"A totally mechanical response!"

Batra shifted his gaze from the window through which he had been peering at the launchers themselves. "Then Space Command is completely correct," he grumbled. "As soon as we figure out how to fix the feedback pulse blockage, we'll be able to give them their errorless, mechanical men!"

Sakchham sat back in his chair, his hands clasped across his moderate stomach. "That is, unfortunately, correct. We've always been mistaken in rejecting Man's mechanistic paradigm. The technologists had suspected it for a long time, but they couldn't prove it. They can now!"

"And Man's soul is nothing more than a feedback impulse!" Sakchham let out a long sigh. "Is there anything else, Batra?"

Swami's Caravan arrived that evening and camped at the military police guards' ten-kilometer limit. They erected protest signs and launched their picket lines. Bakshi dispatched his sound trucks to scare them away, but they were ineffective.

Batra sat at home, watching the drama unfold, but the fate of the Base and the Chakra had almost faded from his mind. He told Shetty about the Hanuman finding Khatri had discovered.

He stated, "It leaves nothing to account for Man's most treasured activities." "Because a cybernetic device can't create, it can only follow a pattern, it can't account for creativity. So, if this is the core of Man, where is the poetry, art, and scientific invention? It can't possibly be, but there's no way to avoid it."

"Where did the pattern come from?" Shetty inquired. "Isn't it a produced thing that the cybernetic system is attempting to emulate?"

With a shake of his head, Batra expressed his dissatisfaction with the situation.

"The pattern we're talking about is nothing more than a mechanical response to stimulus." What we term art, poetry, music inspiration, and intuition, according to Khatri, are nothing more than the outputs of poorly functioning cybernetic systems.

Errors in adapting to the real environment produce more or less irrational outcomes. We enjoy them since they tend to make us forget about our faulty circuits.

"The ideal Man race would be devoid of all of this, a perfectly functioning bunch of humans unaffected by emotional or aesthetic responses, absolutely capable of solving any problem in a purely cybernetic manner."

"Are you in agreement with it?" Shetty inquired.

"I'm at a loss on what to do! The proof is there." He laughed briefly before moving to the window, where he could see Swami's Caravan's neighbouring camp. "Human growth has gone—and continues to go—in a completely different way than I could have imagined.

Bakshi's soulless, iron-hard machine men are the only ones who can get there. The remainder of us who can't keep up with the pace of a technological society will be tossed aside as a byproduct of a race designed to live in galaxies rather than on a single planet."

"I'd have the answer today if I'd ever wondered how you'd sound if you were fully insane," Shetty remarked.

He delegated the responsibility of further identifying and evaluating the feedback impulse they had uncovered to one of the units the next morning. He was summoned to Bakshi's office in the midst of this. Senators in charge of the investigation had arrived.

General Bakshi took them on a day-long tour of the entire base, which they thought was excellent. They found the strongest single factor in favour of allowing Space Command to continue its mission in Batra's announcement.

"We now know that a wholly mechanical man is viable," he continued, "and this is something I haven't even had time to submit to General Bakshi."

As Batra's flat assertion continued, the General's eyes narrowed. "We know that we may have individuals at the helm of our ships who are incapable of making mistakes. If Project Hanuman is allowed to continue, we aim to be able to produce them in a very short period. And once that's done, there's no technical goal we won't be able to achieve."

The Senators were satisfied with the information they received at the base.

"However, the public must be comforted," Senator Pawar stated. "For one thing, we need to move this horde out of your way. The news broadcasts keep them in the public glare all the time, agitating the entire country."

"We'll deal with it right away," General Bakshi stated. "This discovery is so recent, as Dr. Batra has stated, that I was not even aware of it. Swami's horde will disperse as soon as they learn the truth. As a result, the entire country will be reassured. We can arrange for Dr. Batra to provide a national broadcast."

As plans were developed to make a statement to Swami and his group camping outside the Base, the press, and the general public, Batra was carried along.

After the Committee meeting, Bakshi cornered him. "This isn't something you came up with on the spur of the moment?" he asked.

"It's on the same level," Batra added. "All along, you were correct."

When he returned to his office, he was greeted by an urgent message from Sakchham. He dashed down to the testing facility, where the elder guy greeted him with a mixture of eagerness and trepidation.

"It appears that we've caught something by the tail and are unable to release it. Please come in and take a look around."

Captain Iqbal was found writhing on a cot in a storm of tears and emotional rage in an observation room by Batra. His sobbing continued uncontrollably as he slammed his hands against the walls and the floor.

"What happened to him?" Batra was adamant.

"We have three more in the same situation," Sakchham said. "We tried to figure out the effect of a pure feedback impulse by amplifying it and feeding it back to each of them as we found it on their charts. This is how it went down. We don't know why, but I'm worried we may have cost them their sanity."

He wondered aloud, "How could their own feedback do such a thing to them?" "Where did you get it from on the chart?"

"We used the impulse that wasn't able to pass, the one that was impeded, resulting in the error. This appears to be the alternative to making a mistake." He gave a kind nod to the woman.

"Iqbal had to fail or else be subjected to this emotional maelstrom," the writhing, sobbing guy said.

Batra ruffled his hair with his long, bony fingers. "This makes no sense at all!" If that's the case, we'll have to retract what we told Bakshi. After all, his errorless man isn't possible."

"I'm not sure." Sakchham gave a thoughtful shake of his head. "Clearly, the generation of error serves as a deterrent to the acceptance of this unacceptable feedback urge. However, why is it unpleasant, and why does it become such after countless previous feedback impulses have been passed?

"We thought we had it all figured out yesterday." It's now blown open wider than it's ever been!"

***

With the new training techniques that would render men incapable of technical faults, Bakshi's public relations man created a statement to the effect that further danger from pilot error in rocket ships and the second Chakra could be deemed entirely eradicated.

Batra was well aware that it was as ineffective as any other government release, but he raised no objections out of concern for Iqbal and the other three guys. He instantly signed the statement.

The next day, he was presented with plans to personally deliver it to members of Swami's Caravan from the top of one of the sound trucks. He protested at the time, claiming that any flunky on the Base could read it to the throng as well as he could. Bakshi, on the other hand, insisted on doing it himself.

The large, olive-green vehicle moved out of the Base with official grandeur. Batra was seated next to the driver and Sevak, the public relations representative. He hadn't informed Bakshi about their most recent development. If this psychic response to feedback proved impenetrable, there would be enough time to inform Space Command of the bad news. Meanwhile, a Chakra would be constructed, the public would be placated, and Hanuman would move on—to unknown purposes that Batra was unaware of.

Like a discarded rag on either side of the road, the massed camp of Swami's obsessive devotees emerged in the distance. As they got closer, it disintegrated into individual knots of sand-streaked, unwashed people gathering around their tents. Swami hadn't given appropriate facilities any attention before guiding them out here.

The truck came to a complete stop in the middle of the camp. Swami, a long, lanky person dressed in a dusty black suit, led a throng of his followers to greet them. "I hope you have the information we've been waiting for," he remarked warmly.

"We've issued a statement," Sevak remarked. "Dr. Batra will read it to you, since he has made an important discovery that will allow all of you to return to your homes."

Batra might have stayed in the cab, but he decided to scale the truck's platform to survey the audience Swami had gathered. With the document in his hands, he paused for a second before picking up the mike and reading the statement Sevak had prepared. "The Indian

Space Command desires to make the following announcement:"

It fell entirely flat on deafeningly, When Batra gazed at the sea of faces, he realised he'd failed. There was a lot more that was required. He reluctantly considered a little feedback. A little input on their current situation's foolishness to help them change their trajectory and return to normalcy.

"There might have been a mob of people just like you five hundred years ago," he added quietly. "There was a harbour, several small ships, and a man who felt he could sail them over the horizon." On the beach, there were many who felt he was an idiot and a blasphemer, as well as those who believed he was correct—or hoped he was.

"Five hundred years ago, a new freedom from the confines of a small, constrained planet began. Another freedom awaits our triumphant space conquest today. And whenever freedom has been won, there have been more people cheering for it than cheering against it. You will be making a decision today."

He spoke for ten minutes, and when he finished, he knew he'd accomplished his objective. The Caravan's cars were breaking away from the bulk and disappeared in the distance even before the sound truck drew away.

"Nice job," Sevak complimented, as if he'd done it himself.

Batra whispered absently, "Just a little feedback in the appropriate place-" "Feedback? What exactly is this "new type of promotional technique"?"

"That's what you could call it. How could a man be so deaf. "He said it vehemently to himself rather than to his companions.

As soon as the truck returned him to Base, he dashed to the laboratory. Sakchham and Khatri, as well as a dozen of his other senior men, were rounded up. "The answer has always been right in front of our eyes," he explained. "We were too preoccupied with fighting one other for the sake of our own preconceived ideals to notice!"

"Can you tell me what you're talking about?" Khatri was adamant. "Feedback. You haven't figured it out yet, have you?"

"No."

"Are you willing to let us give you a little dose—something less than what Iqbal and his men received—and then report back to us what you learn?"

Khatri had a hesitant expression on his face. "If you believe you have a good understanding of the subject. It's pointless for me to go into Iqbal's situation."

"We'll get you out of there before you get that far."

He took a seat among the pile of pulse generating equipment and electro- encephalograph recorders, still sceptical. His skull was fitted with a single set of feedback terminals. The generator was programmed to replicate his own feedback impulse, which he had recorded during a moment of failure.

Batra gently activated the circuits and advanced the controls. Khatri's face was filled with anguish and regret. With a whimper, he cried out. "Turn it off!"

"Just a second," Batra said. He slid the control forward a smidgeon and waited. The techie burst out crying, his voice low and wailing.

The switch was flipped by Batra.

Khatri remained slumped in his chair for a few period, his shoulders quivering. Then he looked up, half puzzled, half enraged. He shouted, "What did you do to me?"

Batra told him, "You did it to yourself." "Remember, that's your own feedback pulse, just boosted a little. How did it make you feel?"

"Terrible! It's no surprise that a man avoids it. It's enough to make him destroy a space station in order to evade the full force of the blast."

"How would you describe it?"

"I'm not sure—," Khatri paused. "Maybe it's grief. Regret-anxiety. But, I suppose, regret is the most common emotion."

As he withdrew the terminals and went to the others, Batra stated, "That's your feedback."

"These individual feedback pulses are nothing more than stabs of pure passion."

With a small smile, he turned to face Khatri. "You and Iqbal and the rest of the iron-boweled lads were so sure that the pure mechanical man would be free of any emotional responses and substance!" And I was convinced that a warm, responsive, emotional human being could never react in the same way as a frigid machine!

And we were both completely incorrect. The human person is capable of both. He functions according to actual cybernetic principles. The content of his feedback control pulses, on the other hand, is pure emotion!

"A minor blunder, a sting of remorse. It's repeated, intensified, or lessened until the activity returns to the path that leads to the expected outcomes. If the error is ignored, it will worsen until the entire building collapses.

"And we've been taught to disregard it! Ignoring the human sentiments that flood through us is a fine, brave, and manly thing to do. Be anything but a responsive, emotional human being: be steel, glass, or electrons! That's how you become a Hanuman! We've tried everything we can to find the path to perfection and have fought tooth and nail against the only method to get there."

Sakchham's face lit up with delight, and Khatri seemed to recall something from the past. He exhaled quietly, "That was it." "I remember how it felt when I started to grow uneasy and make mistakes during the exam procedures. I seemed to be fighting something inside myself that I believed was causing me to make mistakes. But it wasn't like that. I was battling the emotional feedback that the errors were sending my way."

"Right," Batra agreed. "And your ruthless, error-free Hanuman will be the most emotionally sensitive creature you can create."

"How did you figure this out?" Sakchham enquired.

"We should have seen it in Iqbal,". He is the real Iron Man. He's spent his entire life suppressing and fighting his feelings. The dam was simply shattered by a concentrated dosage of his own feedback.

But it wasn't until I saw Swami's mob react to the completely rational argument Sevak made to persuade them to return home that I realised what was going on.

They were on the wrong track and required a large amount of positive feedback to get back on track. The logical, cool approach failed miserably.

What does it take to persuade an unruly mob emotionally motivated by the expected repercussions of their actions? When used appropriately, this feedback structure is ideal. And it was successful."

Khatri flinched and shifted away from the chair in which he had sat to get a better sense of his own input. He told Batra, "I'm not sure who owes who that supper." "However, I believe someone does."

Batra responded, "We'll share it." Then he became silent as they listened to another cargo ship departing into the thousand-mile orbit, carrying pieces of the second Chakra.

He gave himself a wry grin. He said to himself, "You of little trust!" Fearful of the genuine nature of a race that had endured three billion years of pain similato that which man had endured!

Man had all he needed to travel to the stars or anywhere else he chooses. He was unharmed. Man will never be able to be transformed into a robot. His humanity's basic mechanics were so intertwined with his being's structure that they could never be separated.

But, as Batra knew, they hadn't gotten very far. They had just pried open a small breach in a door that had remained irrationally shut since the dawn of time. They needed to know why that door had never been opened previously. And beyond it, there could be a thousand more that are just as carefully secured and guarded.

Nonetheless, they had finally arrived at a starting place. Project Hanuman could resume its mission of preparing men for space travel.

*****

www.ingramcontent.com/pod-product-compliance
Lightning Source LLC
LaVergne TN
LVHW061559070526
838199LV00077B/7113